W9-AKE-006

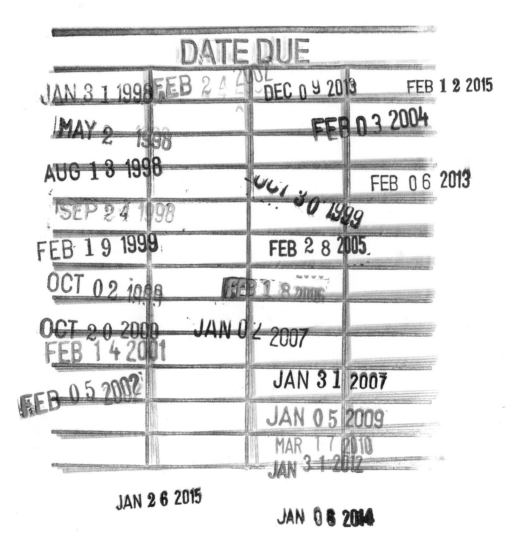

DATE DUE

JAN 3 1 1998	FEB 2 4 2002	DEC 0 9 2013	FEB 1 2 2015
MAY 2 1998		FEB 0 3 2004	
AUG 1 3 1998			FEB 0 6 2013
SEP 2 4 1998		OCT 3 0 1999	
FEB 1 9 1999		FEB 2 8 2005	
OCT 0 2 1998	FEB 1 8 2005		
OCT 2 0 2000	JAN 0 2 2007		
FEB 1 4 2001			
FEB 0 5 2002		JAN 3 1 2007	
		JAN 0 5 2009	
		MAR 1 7 2010	
		JAN 3 1 2012	

JAN 2 6 2015

JAN 0 6 2014

JAN 0 9 2016   JAN 2 5 2016

A WINTER PLACE

A WINTER PLACE

A WINTER PLACE

BY
RUTH YAFFE RADIN

PAINTINGS BY
MATTIE LOU O'KELLEY

LITTLE, BROWN AND COMPANY
BOSTON   TORONTO   LONDON

Library of Congress Cataloging in Publication Data

Radin, Ruth Yaffe.
    A winter place.

    Summary: A family carrying ice skates passes
villages, farms, and forests on the way to a frozen
lake high in the hills. Fifteen paintings accompany
brief descriptive text.
    [1. Ice skating—Fiction. 2. Country life—
Fiction] I. O'Kelley, Mattie Lou, ill. II. Title.
PZ7.R1216Wi   [Fic]   82-15349
ISBN 0-316-73218-4   AACR2

10 9 8 7 6 5 4

JOY STREET BOOKS
ARE PUBLISHED BY
LITTLE, BROWN AND COMPANY (INC.)

AHS

*Published simultaneously in Canada
by Little, Brown & Company (Canada) Limited*

PRINTED IN THE UNITED STATES OF AMERICA

To my mother, Molly
— *Ruth Y. Radin*

To my friends, Fred and Burnice Healan and Lillie Mae Ellison
— *Mattie Lou O'Kelley*

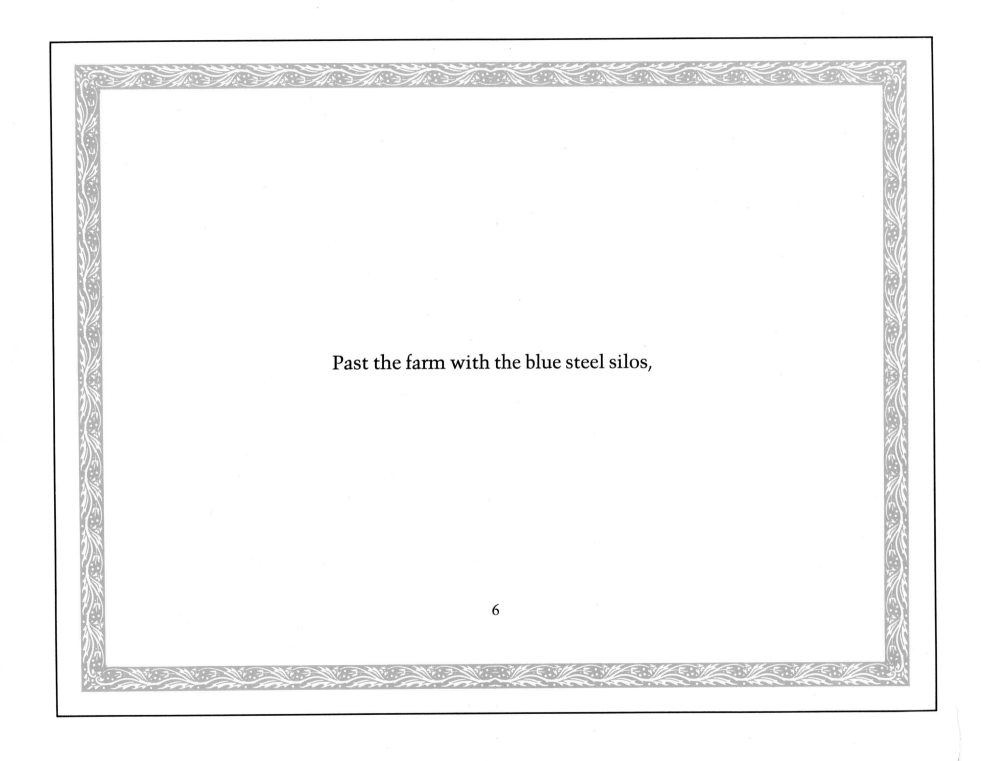

Past the farm with the blue steel silos,

past the racing river at the foot
of the burned-off mountain,

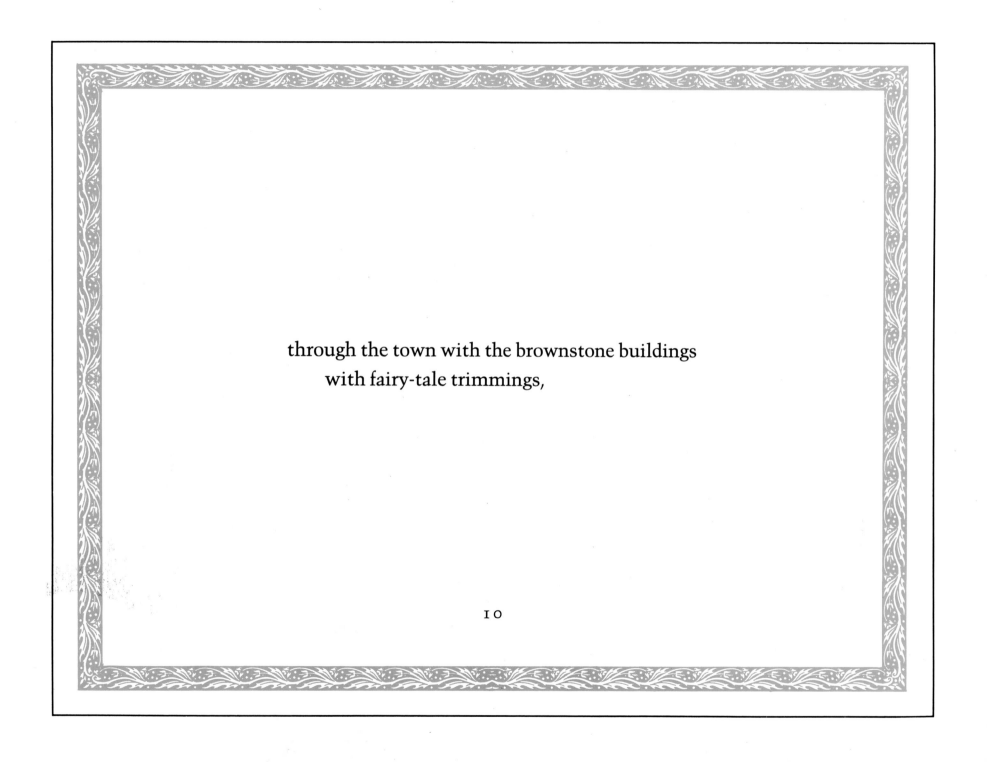

through the town with the brownstone buildings
with fairy-tale trimmings,

there is a special place.

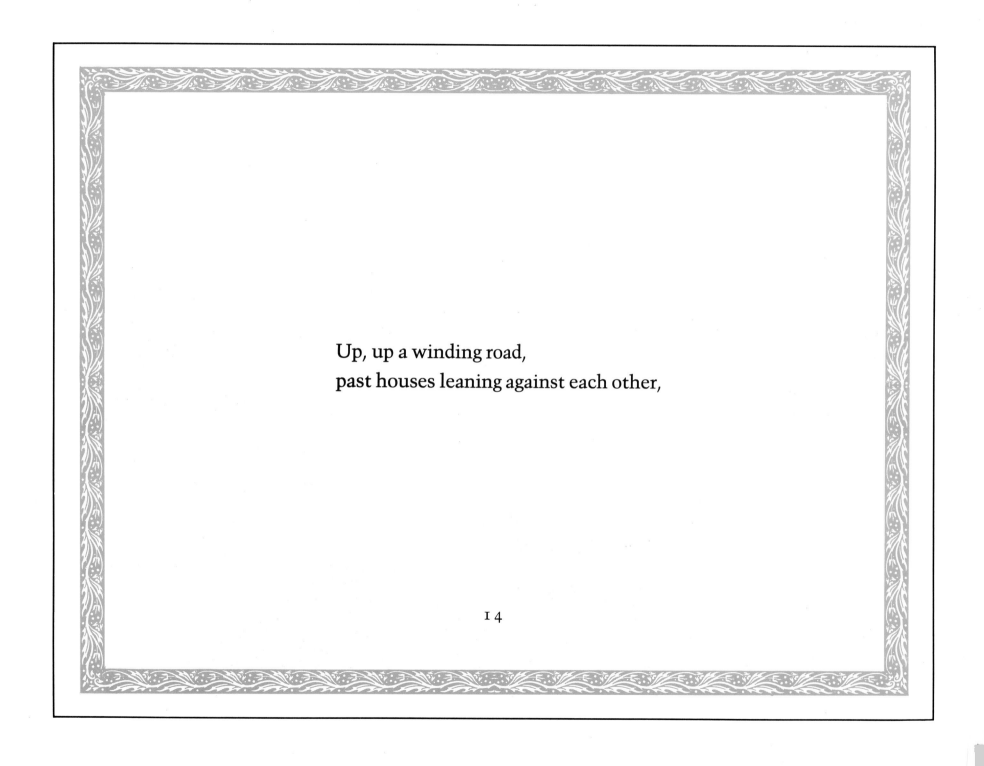

Up, up a winding road,
past houses leaning against each other,

up where trees are free from curbs and corners,

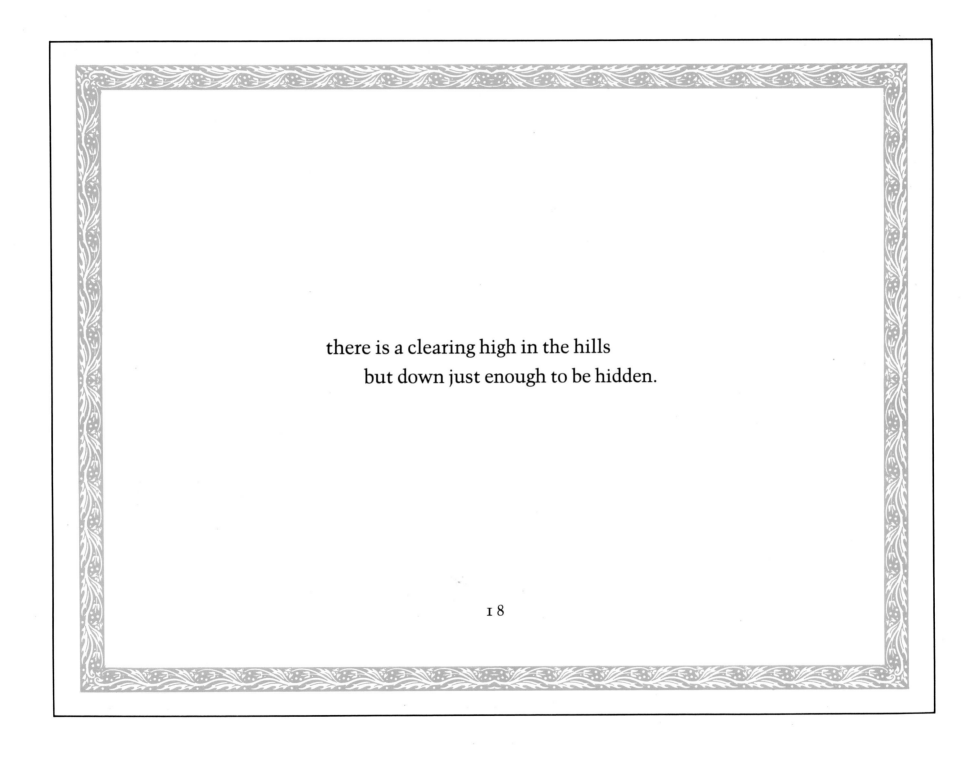

there is a clearing high in the hills
but down just enough to be hidden.

There in the clearing, a long lake is icebound quiet,
except for children calling and falling on the ice,
small sounds for this vast space,
a special place high in the hills for skating,
not around a rink but away,
on blades that swerve around curved snow dustings,
ice fishermen,
frozen footprints and shallow cracks;

a place to break free from a small circle,
go off,
and then come back a new way,
stopping to see a frozen fish on the ice,
stopping to watch a fisherman drill a hole,
stopping to chip away some ice to free a twig,

stopping to see the sun sink behind the hills
and then know it is time to go,
down, down from the hills,

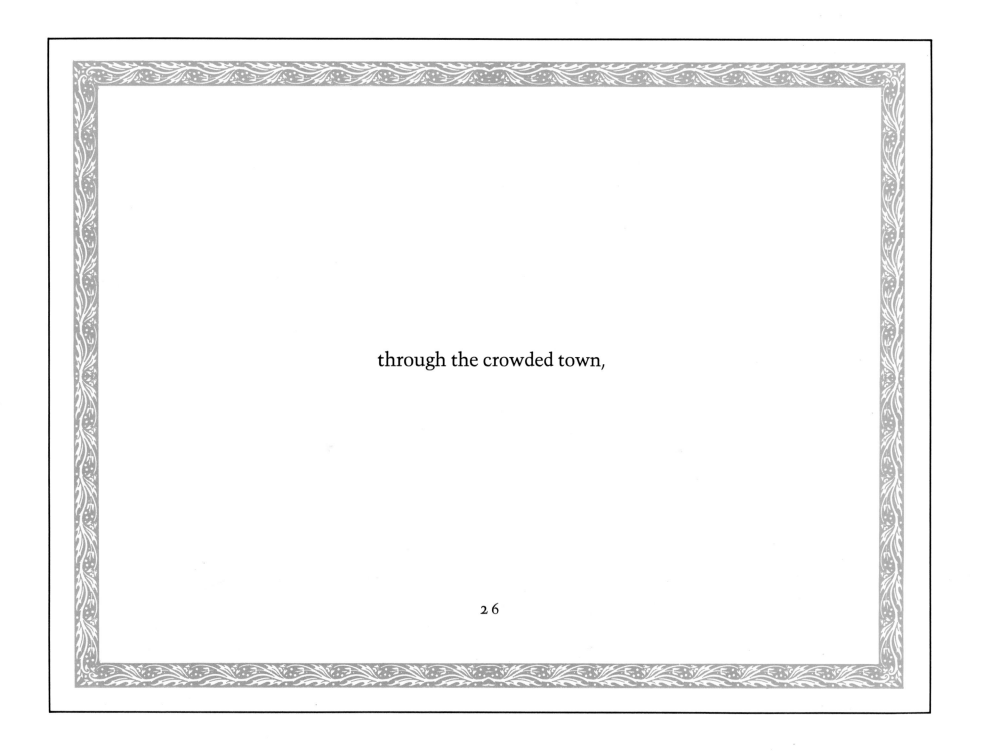

through the crowded town,

past the rushing river
and the silent silos,
to another special place . . .

home.